SAMANTHA
Loses The Box Turtle

by Daisy T. Griffin

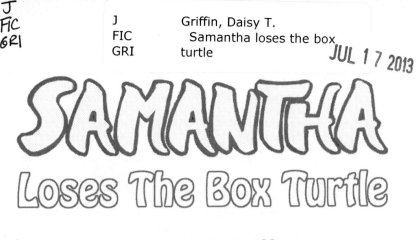

illustrated by Matthew Gauvin

www.SamsAnimals.info

*~For my daughters Laura, Alli, and Charlie, my
constant sources of inspiration ~*

Contents

Chapter 1

Turtle in the Road

"Grampi! Stop the car!"

"What?" Grampi replied as he looked around and started slowing down.

"There's a turtle in the road...stop the car now!" Samantha screamed. Grampi dutifully pulled the car to the side of the road. They had already gone way past the turtle, but Grampi knew from experience that Samantha would not calm down until they had rescued it. Samantha was eight years old and loved animals more than anything else in the world. Especially animals that needed her help.

　　After putting on his emergency lights, Grampi said, "You guys stay in the car, I'll take care of the turtle." Gran, Samantha and her little sister Sophie turned around in their seats to be able to watch and make sure Grampi executed the rescue mission successfully. Samantha and Sophie gasped as another car passed. It came just inches away from turning the turtle into a turtle pancake. As soon as the road was clear, Grampi ran out and grabbed the turtle out of harm's way.

　　At first Samantha was upset because she thought Grampi was going to put it down on the wrong side of the road.

She learned last summer that if you get a turtle out of the road, you should always put it down on the side it was walking toward. Otherwise, the poor thing just has to start over and would go right back into the road again. Grampi was bringing it in the wrong direction!

Before Samantha could object, she heard Gran call out to Grampi, "Oh no you don't! Don't bring that thing is this car, it'll hurt the children, it'll bite us!" Gran was almost to tears and Sophie was giggling as Sam realized that Grampi wasn't putting the turtle down at all. He was bringing it back to the car. A wide grin broke out on Sam's face. She hadn't been very excited about going to the store, but finding a turtle on the way home and getting to keep it made the trip worth it.

"NO NO Noooooooooo!" wailed Gran. Samantha could see that Gran was scared so she tried to calm her down. "Gran it's OK. It's just a box turtle. Mom lets us play with the ones at the nature preserve all the time." Gran was not soothed. She was terrified of all reptiles, whether it was a snake, lizard, or even a turtle. If it was a reptile, Gran didn't like it. Samantha's mom called it a phobia.

Gran had been rummaging around her seat and triumphantly held up a plastic bag. "If you are going to bring that thing into this car, it goes in the bag," she declared. Grampi looked at it skeptically, shrugged his shoulders, and obliged. He carefully lowered the turtle into the bag and started to hand the bag back to the children.

"No you don't," said Gran. "You think it's a nice turtle, but we'll ask their Mom before they can touch it. It could have a disease, or be a different kind than the ones at the preserve. Put it on the floorboard," she said as she pointed to the floorboard at her feet.

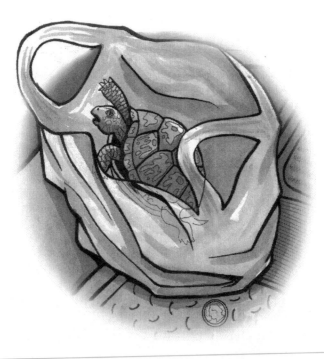

She was worried enough that she wasn't letting it near her grandchildren. This made for an interesting ride home because the turtle was scared of the bag and clawing to get out. Gran was scared of the turtle and screamed every time it moved. Luckily, home wasn't very far away.

Samantha's mom was a zoologist, which means a grown-up who still likes playing with animals. She knew cool stuff about all sorts of animals. Samantha knew as soon as her mom gave the OK, she'd be allowed to play with the new-found turtle. Samantha also knew that it was, in fact, a box turtle. She could have told Gran the scientific name, "*Terrapene carolina*", and whether or not it was male or female. Animals were her thing too, and she had learned a lot from her mom. Sam sighed. Why don't adults ever believe that children know anything?

She was broken out of her thoughts when the car turned into the driveway and came to a stop. Sophie was already out of her booster seat and opening the car door before Samantha could even unbuckle her own seat belt. Sophie was always trying to outdo Samantha. Sam picked up the speed and raced her little sister to be the first to tell their mom. "Grampi got us a turtle!" they both yelled at once. They were in the middle of telling their mom all about the heroic rescue and how funny Gran's screaming was when Grampi walked in with the turtle.

"We found him in the middle of town. There wasn't a safe place to put

8

him so we brought him home. I figured you would know what to do with him," Grampi grinned. Samantha knew he was having fun with this too.

Chapter 2

Greenish Brown Rock

Gran was still keeping her distance as Samantha begged her mom to say she could play with the turtle. "What a lovely surprise," Mom said, "but your Gran was right to be careful. Let's just see what we have here." Mom tried to hide her amusement as she gently untangled the turtle from the, now mangled, plastic bag. She looked closely all over the turtle, examining his head, legs and shell completely. Samantha suspected her mom was mostly concerned about making sure he wasn't hurt.

After the inspection her Mom said, "He looks quite healthy, and he's definitely an eastern box turtle. Hasn't tried to bite either. Girls you may keep an eye on him while I get a box ready." Sophie reached up and tried to grab the turtle from their Mom before Samantha could, but Mom was too smart for that. "Uh uh, we aren't going to get into a fight over who holds the turtle. Let the little guy walk around. He's probably more comfortable on the floor anyway."

Samantha and Sophie both groaned, but sat down with their legs spread out across from each other and their feet touching with the turtle in the middle. At first, he just sat there. Sat there like a brownish green rock. Once he became the subject of scrutiny, the turtle pulled its head, legs, and even its tail up into the shell. There was absolutely no movement at all.

Just then they heard, "Tuttle, tuttle." Mom had just unstrapped their baby sister from the highchair and let her loose.

Michelle toddled over to see the turtle. Before they could stop her she had gone right over their protective leg barrier and started poking at the closed up turtle.

"No silly," said Samantha, "turtle scared. He thinks you want to eat him so he's hiding in his shell."

"I no eat tuttle. bleh!" Michelle declared as she stuck out her tongue in disgust. Just then Michelle saw that Grampi was sitting down with a bag of chips so she left the still quiet turtle in favor of more promising rewards.

Slowly, just when Samantha and Sophie were starting to get bored of watching, the box turtle started to peek out from his shell. He let his head and legs come out and had only taken one step before Sophie reached over and grabbed him. The head and legs disappeared instantly. "Sophie! You scared him," said Samantha.

"Oops. I thought he was ready to play with me," grinned Sophie.

"Next time, just don't touch him. OK?"

"OK."

It didn't take quite as long this time for the box turtle to unbox. Sophie made a move to grab him, but Samantha glared at her and she sat on her hands sheepishly. Both sisters waited to see what he would do. Samantha hoped that he would walk over to her. After he had been out for a few seconds and no one touched him, the box turtle started walking. Fast. He did his little turtle run right into Samantha's leg and started trying to climb it. Sophie looked ready to burst to try to get him to crawl on her. Samantha tried not to gloat, but she couldn't help the smile that pulled at the corners of her mouth. Sophie would get her chance later, but the turtle crawled to Samantha first.

When he started being successful in his attempts to climb, Samantha gently picked him up and turned him in the other direction. By then the turtle seemed to understand that the girls weren't really going to hurt him and only pulled his head in a little bit when she touched him. As soon as he was on the floor, he was off to a run again. The girls played guess-who-the-turtle-will-tag-next until their mom came back with one of the large plastic bins that usually held out of season clothes in the attic. Now instead of clothes, the bottom of it was covered with a deep layer of pine straw from their backyard. "Why'd you put so much pine straw in there? He's going to get lost," Sophie asked their Mom.

"That's the point," Mom replied, "Box turtles like to burrow or dig down under the leaves and pine straw. It keeps them hidden from predators that would eat them, and keeps them warmer. He'll feel safer if he can dig down."

"But then I won't be able to see him. He's already safe here. I don't think he needs the pine straw," Sophie whined. Samantha knew her mom was right and she wanted the turtle to be happy.

"You are safe in your bed too, but you still wouldn't want to sleep without

Purple Bunny would you?" Sam told her. Sophie was quiet after that. She never ever slept without Purple Bunny.

Chapter 3

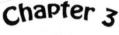

What's in a Name?

"What should we name him?" Samantha wondered.

"Box Turtle #1," her mom said.

"Mom! That's not a name," she groaned.

"We could name him Shelly, because he has a shell," Sophie offered.

"That's almost as bad as Box Turtle #1," said Sam.

"Guys, I'm serious," Mom interjected, "he doesn't get a name. As friendly and cute as he is, he's a wild animal and we'll be letting him go tomorrow."

"Can't we keep him Mom?" they asked.

"Absolutely not!" replied their mother. "Turtles take a lot of care and we don't have the right kind of habitat for him." The girls sighed. They were just about to start arguing that they could make a habitat for him when their mom said, "Well I do know somewhere with a very nice turtle habitat. Somewhere that he would be taken care of, but we could still visit him. Somewhere liiiike..."

"The Nature Preserve!" the girls both shouted. That was perfect, well, not quite perfect. Perfect would have been keeping him in their bedroom, but at least this way they could still see him. It also gave them another excuse to go visit the Nature Preserve which they always loved.

"If he lives at the Preserve he still needs a name," Samantha pointed out happily.

"So we'll know what to call him when we go visit," Sophie chimed in.

"Fair enough," Mom agreed, "What can we call him?"

Just then Michelle came toddling back over to see what was happening. Grampi and Gran were getting ready to leave and her chip supply had run out. "Where tuttle?" she said as she looked into the box. Samantha looked into the box, but all she saw was pine straw. She had a moment of panic, then she remembered the reason the pine straw was there to begin with. "He's hiding,"

Sam told Michelle. Then she reached with her hand down into the pine straw until she felt something hard and lifted out the turtle. Michelle clapped.

"Seek, hide. Seek, hide," she said, wanting to play hide and seek with the turtle.

"I'm afraid not, little one. You have to get ready for bed," Dad said as he came in and swooped up Michelle.

Grampi and Gran came by and gave each of the girls a kiss before they headed out to go home. They lived next door, so they didn't have far to go. It was nice having them close by. Samantha was really glad she got to see them every day. Her other grandparents lived a long way away so she didn't get to visit them very often. She did get to talk to them on the computer though and this was a perfect time to use the video chat. As Sophie walked Gran and Grampi to the door, Samantha ran to the computer and clicked to call Grandma and Grandpa. She only had to wait a minute before she saw Grandma's face on the other end.

"Hey Samantha, did you call to tell us goodnight?" Grandma asked.

"Yep, and I have a surprise for you." Samantha was already holding the turtle in her hands so she lifted him up in front of the camera.

"Oh, she's a beauty," said Grandma.

"Grandma not she...he," Sam corrected.

"Well, how are you so sure?" asked Grandma. She knew Samantha did know

the difference, and Grandma was good
about giving opportunities to show off.

Samantha took her cue and started explaining, "Here, look at the plastron, the bottom of his shell. See how there is a dip in it? Like someone pushed his belly in with a spoon. Only boys have that."

"It's so they can get on top of the girls!" Sophie blurted out laughing. She heard Grandma and had come to talk. Their mom had told them earlier why the boy turtles had a dip in the shell on their belly and the thought of one turtle climbing onto another turtle's back sent Sophie into fits of laughter.

"Also," Samantha continued in her most mature voice to try to win back the conversation, "his eyes are red. Boy box turtles have red eyes and girl box turtles have brown eyes. Or usually they do anyway."

"I stand corrected," laughed Grandma, "*He* is a beauty. What is *his* name?"

"He doesn't have one yet," said Sam.

"Boxer!" said Grandpa, as he joined the conversation. "You should name him Boxer, because he's a BOX turtle! HA HA!" Grandpa laughed at his own joke. He never missed an opportunity to make a cheesy joke.

"Grandpa!" Samantha laughed and groaned all at the same time, "He needs a real name, not a joke."

"Fine, how about George?" he offered. Samantha shook her head no. That still wasn't quite right. Surprisingly, the perfect name came from silly Sophie.

"Let's call him Gayzer!" she said.

"Gayzer?" asked Sam.

25

"Cause we found him on Gay street....and I like the sound ZER," replied Sophie matter-of-factly.

"I like it," said Sam. Grandma and Grandpa agreed and so their newly found box turtle was named Gayzer.

"Mom, do you think I could take Gayzer to school tomorrow before we take him to the Nature Preserve?" Samantha asked right before she crawled into bed. "We're studying the food chain in science. I could talk about what he eats and what eats him," Samantha persuaded.

"I don't know, honey," Mom started to say.

"Pleeeeeease. I'll take good care of him and won't let anyone hurt him. You are always saying that more kids need to get to know animals. Please, please, pleeeease!" Mom sighed. She knew perfectly well that Samantha's true reason for taking the turtle to school was to show him off to her friends, but she did make a convincing argument. The truth was, Mom thought it was a good idea to. She just didn't know what the school policy was on bringing live animals to the classroom.

"Tell you what, Sam. I'll give Mrs. Klutz a call tonight and see if it's even allowed. If it's OK with her, it's OK with me."

"Thank you! Thank you!" Samantha squealed.

"Uh huh," Mom mumbled. "Now get some rest." Samantha went to sleep happy and excited for tomorrow. If only she had known what was coming.

Chapter 4

To Take a Turtle to School

The next morning Samantha's eyes flew open and she climbed down from the top bunk in record time. She knew before bedtime tonight she would have to let Gayzer go at the Nature Preserve and she wanted to spend all the time she could with him.

As she was rummaging around in the pine straw to find him, Michelle toddled into the room laughing, "hide seek tuttle, hide seek tuttle."

"Yep and I'm going to find him and play with him," Samantha smiled as she replied.

"Tuttle hide seek, tuttle hide seek," Michelle went on chanting. Samantha kept searching in the pine straw, but she soon came to realize that the box turtle was not in the plastic bin where she left him last night. Sophie must have beaten her awake, so Sam went to go find her. When she passed by Sophie's bed, however, Sophie was still sound asleep complete with a little dribble of drool out the side of her mouth. Sophie could sleep through anything.

Samantha felt a moment of panic. Maybe her mom had already gotten Gayzer ready for school. Sam went into the kitchen where mom was fixing breakfast. "Mom, how are we going to carry Gayzer today?" Samantha asked as innocently as she could. If Mom didn't know Gayzer was missing she didn't want to tell her. Mom needed to think she was responsible if she was going to let Sam take Gayzer to school. Losing him first thing in the morning was not responsible.

"You can put him in the cat carrier dear. Mrs. Klutz did say you could bring him. I'll help you when I finish getting breakfast ready," Mom replied.

"Uh oh", Samantha thought. Mom didn't know where the box turtle was, and now she only had until breakfast was ready to find him. She ran back into the room she shared with her two sisters. Sophie was still snoozing on the bottom bunk, and Michelle was playing over by the toy box. Dad had already headed out for work, so he didn't have the turtle. Samantha walked over to the plastic bin and searched through the pine straw one more time. She just couldn't figure out how he could get out on his own. Then she heard Michelle's singing again, "Hide seek tuttle!" Samantha looked up and saw the toys in the toy box moving around on their own a bit.

"Michelle!" Sam laughed as she walked over to the toy box, "The turtle doesn't play hide and seek in the toys, only in the pine straw."

Michelle's lip quivered for a moment and she looked like she was about to cry. Then the turtle peeked his head out of the pile of toys. Michelle giggled like crazy, pointed, and started saying, "Yes does.

Look. Hide seek tuttle!" Samantha couldn't help but laugh as she dug the poor turtle out of the toys.

"Good thing you have a tough shell to protect you from little sisters," Samantha told Gayzer. Gayzer didn't look too worried.

Samantha put Gayzer in the cat carrier. Well, it was supposed to be for cats, but it had been used for snakes, ferrets, lizards and today a turtle. She packed it half full of pine straw before she put Gayzer in. There was also a bag with a water pan and food bowl in it. Samantha was supposed to set that up once she got to school so that it didn't get messy during transport. All in all it wasn't hard to carry and Samantha insisted that her Mom could drop her off as usual. No need to walk her in.

Chapter 5

Box Turtles Won't Bite

As soon as she got out of the car at school Samantha spotted her best friend, Gerti. Gerti's real name was Gertrude, but she hated her real name. So everyone called her Gerti. She was super shy and sensitive. Samantha and Gerti had been best friends since kindergarten. "Hey, Gerti! Check out what I've got. We found him in the road yesterday and Mrs. Klutz said I could bring him to class," Samantha hollered out to her friend.

Gerti smiled as she saw Samantha coming over, but she slowed down as soon as she saw the pet carrier. Gerti knew from experience that you never know what kind of animal Samantha might be carrying. In the first grade Gerti had looked into a pet carrier that Samantha was carrying expecting to see a cat and saw a snake instead. Gerti was scared of snakes. She had not forgotten that experience.

Samantha noticed her hesitation and said, "Don't worry Gert, it's just a turtle."

"Turtles bite," Gerti replied.

Samantha laughed, "Gerti. Do you think I would bring a turtle that would bite to school?"

"Yes!"

Samantha sighed. She kinda deserved that, but it was still frustrating that her best friend didn't trust her. Sam said, "Snapping turtles are the ones that will bite you....and soft shell turtles and probably a few other species I guess...but this, this is a box turtle. Totally sweet, not aggressive at all. I played with him all last night. Promise."

Gerti approached the pet carrier slowly and peeked in. "I don't see anything," she said.

"Drats, I forgot he'd burrowed down. Hold on a sec," Samantha said as she started to open the carrier to pull him out.

"Sam, please don't open it. I'll see the turtle in class," Gerti insisted. Just then Josh, the class bully, was walking by and heard the word turtle.

Josh stopped walking and asked, "You've got a turtle in there? Let me hold him."

Suddenly Samantha didn't want to get Gayzer out anymore. Josh did mean things sometimes and Sam didn't trust him at all.

"Sorry, can't let anyone hold him unless the teacher says it's OK," Samantha told him.

"You were going to let Gerti! So you can let me. I just want to hold him once," Josh retorted.

"I was only trying to show him to Gerti. No one else but me can touch him unless Mrs. Klutz says so," Samantha said. She actually had promised her mom that very thing this morning before she was allowed to bring Gayzer to school. Even though she had forgotten it until Josh tried to take Gayzer, it was still the truth. Samantha was glad she had that excuse because she didn't want Josh touching Gayzer.

Josh's friend Derek came over and also begged to touch him, but Samantha pushed through until she got to the classroom. Gerti was afraid of Josh so she shied away and went to her desk as soon as she was sure that Samantha was OK. Mrs. Klutz was expecting the turtle and told Samantha to get Gayzer's cage set up on the floor by her desk. Josh stopped pestering Sam as soon as they got in the classroom. He headed over to the coat rack and dumped his coat on the floor.

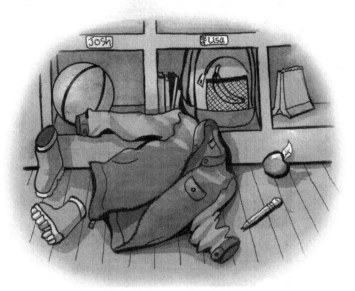

There was a peg for every student, but Josh never seemed to bother actually hanging his coat up. Apparently on the floor *near* the hooks was good enough.

Another girl, Lisa, came over to try to help with the turtle setup. Lisa was always in the center of anything going on. It didn't really matter if she was needed or not. Samantha set the cage on the floor. Then she sent Lisa to get some water for the water dish and put it in the carrier as well. Samantha was going to put in some apples in case Gayzer got hungry, but Mrs. Klutz took the apples and said she wanted to save them for later.

The class started with their normal morning work, but word quickly passed around that there was a turtle in the room. It was hard for everyone to focus when they wanted to see the turtle. Luckily, science came early in the day and it wasn't long before it was time to get Gayzer out.

Chapter 6

What Eats a Box Turtle?

First Mrs. Klutz had everyone push the desks back out of the middle of the room. Then she told them to sit in a circle. It took a minute for all the kids to settle down. Josh and Derek were shoving one another and Lisa seemed to keep changing her mind about where she should sit. Mrs. Klutz picked up the animal carrier and walked to the middle of the circle. She only had to wait a moment before everyone was silent. They knew from experience that she wouldn't say a word until they all gave her their attention. They also knew that she was worth paying attention to. First she went around the circle and laid one card face down in front of each student. Then she walked back to the middle. "Who can tell me what we've been studying in science?" Mrs. Klutz's voice rang out.

Everyone's hand shot up in the air. Mrs. Klutz pointed to a boy named Joe. "The food chain," Joe said eagerly.

"Very good. Our turtle friend here is a living creature. As such, he is part of the food chain, like every other living plant and animal," Mrs. Klutz began. She reached into the carrier and pulled out Gayzer.

As she held him up so everyone could see she said, "This turtle must eat food in order to survive. If it does not eat, then it will die. In the same way, there are other animals that may try to eat this turtle because they too, are hungry."

"In front of each of you is a card. You may pick it up and look at it," Mrs. Klutz said. Everyone grabbed their cards and looked to see what was on them. There were pictures of different kinds of plants and animals. Mrs. Klutz then handed Gayzer to Samantha and said, "When you are holding the turtle I want you to show everyone your card. Tell us if you think the thing on the card would eat a turtle, or be eaten by a turtle, or neither." Samantha looked at her card. It was a mushroom and Samantha knew that turtles ate mushrooms. She held the card up for everyone to see, then took a minute and pretended to think about it. She didn't want to pass Gayzer on too quickly, after all. "Mushrooms would be eaten by a turtle," Samantha finally said.

"Excellent! They would indeed." said Mrs. Klutz.

"Some mushrooms are poisonous. I bet they wouldn't eat the poisonous ones," Lisa butted in. Samantha rolled her eyes. She knew she shouldn't, but she couldn't help it. Lisa was always trying to act like she knew everything.

"Very good question," Mrs. Klutz said.

"It wasn't really a question," Samantha mumbled under her breath.

Luckily no one but Gerti heard, and she only giggled a little.

Mrs. Klutz continued, "Box turtles actually *do* eat the poisonous mushrooms as well. The poison doesn't hurt the turtle. It stays inside them. That way if a predator eats the turtle it will poison the predator. It's a sneaky way for the turtle to use the mushroom's defense for himself."

"Cool," said Joe.

"Very cool, indeed! Now Samantha, will you please pass the turtle to Gerti and let her show us her card?" Mrs. Klutz prompted.

Sam gladly handed Gayzer to Gerti, who stood up as she took him a bit gingerly. Gerti still wasn't enthused about touching a reptile of any sort. When she held up her card Gerti showed everyone a skunk.

"Pee U," someone shouted.

"Nothing would want to get close to a skunk," came another remark. Mrs. Klutz held up her hand for silence and the room quieted down.

Gerti was quite for a minute, then finally said, "I don't think this turtle could eat a skunk, but I don't know if a skunk would eat a turtle either. I don't really know what a skunk might eat, but I'm going to guess the skunk would eat the turtle."

"Very good deduction, Gerti. Skunks do eat turtles along with just about anything else small enough for them to get their claws into.

But are you certain that a turtle wouldn't eat a skunk as well?" Mrs. Klutz prompted.

Gerti looked at the box turtle in her hand. He was full grown and not quite as big as a football. The skunk she had seen at the zoo was bigger than her beagle, Ruby. She couldn't figure out how the sweet little turtle would manage to get a bite out of a big skunk.

"He'd have to be one crazy turtle to kill a skunk," Gerti finally answered. Everyone laughed.

"Ah ha, but what if the skunk were already dead? What then?" prodded Mrs. Klutz. That was what made Mrs. Klutz such a fun teacher. She never made fun of your answers, or made you feel stupid;

but she always made you try a little harder and think a little deeper.

"If the skunk were already dead, I guess the turtle *could* eat it...but I don't know if he would *want* to," Gerti replied.

Mrs. Klutz said, "Good answer Gerti. In fact, box turtles have been known to scavenge. That's what it's called when one animal eats another animal that it finds already dead."

And so it went as one by one every student in the class got to hold a very patient box turtle. Yes, he would eat a strawberry. No, he wouldn't eat a tree. A dog or a cat would probably eat a box turtle, but a turtle would eat an earthworm. At the end, after the last student declared that box turtles would love to eat peaches, Mrs. Klutz placed

Gayzer on the floor in the center of the circle of students. By this time, he had become quite calm with being handled and wasn't closing up in his shell at all.

Then the teacher placed an apple slice in front of Gayzer and he started happily munching away.

Watching a turtle eat sounds like about as much fun as watching grass grow, but it was really kinda cool. Everyone scooted as close as they could to get a look. Gayzer, very matter-of-factly ignored them all and enjoyed his apple.

Once he stopped eating Mrs. Klutz let Josh put him back in the carrier and said that it was time to move on to math. The entire class groaned....well, almost the entire class. Gerti gave a sigh of relief. Gerti was really good at math and couldn't get enough of it. Turtles on the other hand still made her a little nervous.

Josh hung around the carrier petting Gayzer until Mrs. Klutz told him sternly to hurry up or he would spend recess doing math. That threat got him moving and he shut the carrier door in a hurry. Mrs.

Klutz didn't make idle threats and Josh didn't want to spend his recess time inside doing math.

Chapter 7

One Minus One Equals Zero

Today's math lesson was a short one. They were reviewing multiplication tables before they moved on to division. Samantha had been practicing her multiplication tables every day at home so she knew them really well. It made the lesson easy to keep up with. Gerti practiced even more than Samantha, so she was bored with the lesson. They passed the time writing notes back and forth and before they knew it, it was time for recess. Everyone was happy to head outside. Unfortunately just as they were about to walk out the door it started raining. Not just raining, but pouring. It was like someone had turned on a waterfall over the top of the school.

"Back to the classroom," Mrs. Klutz informed them. Samantha stared out at the rain disappointedly. They had been planning a kickball game at recess, now they'd have to sit around inside. Oh well, maybe Mrs. Klutz would let her get Gayzer out again, she thought. By the time Samantha had turned around, most of her classmates were already down the hallway and heading into the classroom. Samantha followed them.

Mrs. Klutz was opening the window so everyone could enjoy the "fresh rainy air" as Samantha walked back in the room.

Samantha walked over to the teacher and asked, "Would it be alright if I got the box turtle out during recess?"

"That would be fine, Sam, just be careful that he doesn't get hurt," Mrs. Klutz responded. Other kids were already gathering in groups, setting up board games or generally finding other ways to amuse themselves for recess. Samantha headed straight for the turtle carrier. When she reached down to open the door to the carrier, she was surprised to find that it wasn't latched. The door was swinging open freely.

"Oh no!" she cried as she reached down into the pine straw. She felt around, desperately hoping that he had just burrowed himself down deep inside the cage. No luck.

Samantha pulled out every bit of pine straw right there on the floor and went through it all, just in case she was missing him. No turtle.

Josh heard the commotion and walked up behind her. He said, "Here's a math lesson. What's one turtle minus one turtle? Zero."

Samantha felt her cheeks go red. Stealing a turtle was just the sort of thing Josh would do and he had been back in the classroom before her.

Samantha whirled around and screamed, "What did you do with him Josh?"

"Me? I didn't take the turtle, isn't he there?" Josh replied. He actually did look innocent, but he was probably good at pretending to be innocent.

"No he's not here! The door was open and he's gone." Samantha held up a fistful of pine straw to make her point. "Gone!" she said again narrowing her eyes at him.

"Sam, I promise, I didn't take him. I
thought he was just hiding in the pine
straw. I wouldn't hurt the turtle. I like
him," Josh said.

By this time, Mrs. Klutz had heard the commotion and come over to check on them. Most of the other students in the class were watching as well. The teacher took a moment to assess the situation. She had heard Samantha and Josh's argument and saw the empty carrier and the pine straw all over the floor.

Mrs. Klutz turned and addressed the class as a whole, "Our box turtle friend has escaped from his cage. I need everyone to help find him." Students started looking around and getting up. Mrs. Klutz held up her hand and waited until she had everyone's attention again. She continued, "I want you all to be very careful of where you step while we are searching. If you step on his shell it will hurt the turtle. Shauna and Alex, will you please go and check the hallway in case he walked out while our door was open? Joe and Carter, can the two of you look in the bathroom? Samantha, you and Josh can clean up this pine straw and get his cage ready again. Everyone else please search the classroom carefully."

All the students went into action immediately. Samantha felt better. He was just a turtle, after all. He couldn't have gone far and everyone was looking for him. They should find him soon. Unless, Josh really did take him. She still wasn't sure.

Chapter 8

Predator in the Classroom

"Look, it's Ms. Kitty," Lisa cooed. Ms. Kitty was a stray cat that came by the classroom sometimes to say hello. She came because she knew that Mrs. Klutz had a tray of food on the window sill, but she never ever let anyone touch her. Mrs. Klutz said that Ms. Kitty was born and raised wild and had learned not to trust humans. She had started to warm up to Mrs. Klutz a little bit, but a few weeks ago Mrs. Klutz had trapped the cat. She had done it to take Mrs. Kitty to the vet to be spayed and get her shots so she'd be healthy. Afterwards the teacher had released Ms. Kitty again. This was the first time they had seen her since. Apparently hunger had finally gotten the better of her and she had come back to find an easy meal.

Even though Ms. Kitty wasn't a pet, she was always a welcome diversion at the window. Normally, the windowsill was as far as she got. Today, however, the window was open and it was raining outside so after a few moments of eating out of her dish, Ms. Kitty hopped down into the classroom.

Samantha smiled when she saw the cat. Sam had been worried that something bad had happened to her or that she had been spooked away forever. Samantha's happiness in the moment was shattered, however, when Gerti leaned over and said, "Um, Sam. Wasn't a cat one of the predators that eats turtles?" Samantha got a tight knot in her stomach. Cats *could* eat turtles. Especially a cat that was wild and hungry.

Josh happened to be nearby and heard Gerti's comment. He yelled out, "Ms. Kitty's gonna eat the turtle!" In that moment, several things seemed to happen all at once. Lisa went from cooing over Ms. Kitty to shooing her. Mary and Carter, who had been standing close to where Ms. Kitty had jumped down, both lunged to grab the cat at once. Ms. Kitty sensed a trap again and dodged them with a graceful leap out of the way. Instead of catching the cat, Mary and Carter knocked each other in the head. "Ouch!" Mary cried out. Carter tried to look tough, but he was rubbing his head.

Their failed attempt seemed to spur everyone else into action and the room erupted in students chasing the cat. Ms. Kitty went straight for the window and Samantha thought she was going to jump out and away without any trouble. Just when she got there, though, the cat took one look at the pouring rain and decided she'd rather take her chances with the third graders. Back into the classroom Ms. Kitty leaped and landed on the teacher's desk. Derek was right behind her trying to grab her tail. Ms. Kitty was too fast for him and jumped again knocking a vase of flowers onto the floor.

The vase shattered and water and flowers spilled out all over the floor. This only spurred the cat into a higher state of frenzy.

"Enough!" Mrs. Klutz's voice rang out. The cat had gone for high ground. She managed to jump up onto some high cabinets while the children below her were still running around chasing each other.

When they heard Mrs. Klutz everyone stopped and looked around. The room was in shambles. One girl was sitting in the floor crying. Josh sheepishly got down from on top of the table where he had been standing to try to get the jump on the cat and tried to look nonchalant.

Chapter 9

Think Like a Turtle

"Now," said Mrs. Klutz, "We have gotten ourselves into quite a mess." She looked around sternly. Mrs. Klutz was giving them her angry look, but Samantha could almost swear the teacher's eyes were laughing.

"Sorry, Mrs. Klutz, but we had to save the turtle," Josh piped up. Samantha was surprised at how sincere he seemed. She was starting to think maybe, just maybe, he wasn't the culprit after all.

"I see. A very noble thought Josh." Mrs. Klutz lost her angry look and the smile broke through as she said, "I think perhaps we can save the turtle *and* keep from traumatizing our friend Ms. Kitty any further. She is a guest here too, after all. Lisa and Gerti, would you please keep an eye on Ms. Kitty and make sure that she doesn't discover a turtle shaped snack?" Mrs. Klutz asked. The girls both nodded and began to intently stare at the cat. No turtle would be devoured on their watch. Ms. Kitty seemed content to stay high above the bothersome children.

"Peter, will you and Carter get the broom and dustpan and very carefully clean up this mess that my vase has become?" Mrs. Klutz asked of two of the boys in the class. They too nodded yes

and went straight to work. Mrs. Klutz
looked around the room. "As for
everyone else, please start straightening
up everything else that was disturbed
during our cat chase. While you are
cleaning, I want everyone to try to think of
where you would hide if you were a
turtle."

Samantha started to clean up like all
the other kids. She grabbed some papers
that had fallen to the floor and put them
back on the desk.

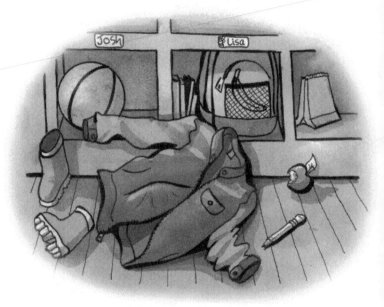

Josh's coat was lying on the floor,
but that wasn't caused by the commotion,
it was always on the floor. Samantha left
it, but she picked up a backpack that had
gotten knocked off the hook and hung it
back neatly. As she worked she kept
trying to think where Gayzer could
possibly be hiding.

The kids looked everywhere they could think of. The floor in the classroom, the bathroom, even the hallway. Gayzer was definitely not in his cage. They made sure of that. He had tricked her so many times by burrowing down that Samantha had taken out all of the pine straw just to make sure. All of a sudden, a light-bulb went on in Samantha's head. "Burrowing!" she shouted out loud. Everyone looked up as Samantha ran over to where Josh's coat had been laying in the floor all day. She very carefully picked up the coat and inside she found Gayzer who had been laying there fast asleep.

Cheers filled the room. Josh ran over and stood beside Samantha, looking close to make sure Gayzer wasn't hurt.

"You did it Sam!" he shouted. Samantha thought maybe Josh wasn't so bad after all.

Mrs. Klutz looked pleased. "Now Samantha, however did you figure out where he was?" the teacher asked.

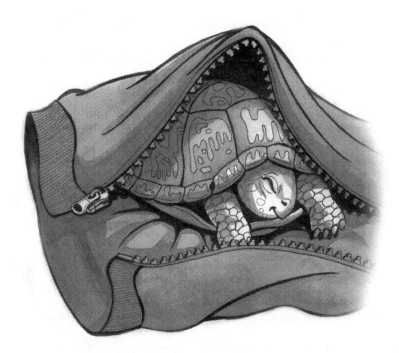

"Simple," Samantha replied, "I started thinking about how he always burrows in the pine straw. Then it hit me, if a box turtle wants to hide he'd try to burrow. The only thing he could burrow into in this room was Josh's coat."

"What a wonderful deduction Samantha," Mrs. Klutz praised her, "I'm glad Gayzer is safe and sound." With that she took the box turtle from Samantha and put him back in his cage. This time she made sure the door was truly latched.

"What about Ms. Kitty?" Gerti asked shyly.

"Well, with the turtle in his cage, I don't see any harm in letting her stay in out of the rain for a while. I'll leave the window open until she decides to head out," Mrs. Klutz replied.

Chapter 10

Turtle Tag

Samantha and Gerti waited in the car line for their moms to pick them up from school. Gerti asked Samantha, "So what happens to Gayzer now? Are you going to let him go?"

"My mom is taking me to the Nature Preserve after school. They have a box turtle habitat there where he can live," Samantha replied.

"Can I come along?" Gerti asked.

"Sure. You ask your mom when you get in the car, and I'll get my mom to stop by your house on our way there," Samantha said. Having Gerti come along would be great. Samantha was always trying to get Gerti to come out to the Nature Preserve, but this is the first time she said she wanted to.

When Samantha's Mom picked her up she already had Sophie and Michelle in the car. There was also a bag full of apple slices for a snack. Things were all set to head to the Preserve. As soon as she had herself buckled in and Gayzer settled, Samantha said, "Mom, Gerti wants to come along when we take Gayzer to the Nature Preserve. Can we pick her up on our way?"

"Sure, honey. I'll call her mom right now," Mom replied as she picked up the cell phone and pressed Gerti's number.

"I wanna hold Gayzer while we ride," Sophie called out from the back seat of the van. Samantha hesitated. She didn't want to give him to Sophie, but she knew she should. "I haven't seen him all day. Give me a turn," Sophie begged.

"Alright, but I get him back when we get there," Samantha said as she took Gayzer out of the carrier and handed him back to Sophie.

After picking up Gerti, the group headed out to the Nature Preserve. Samantha's Mom had talked to the Director of the Preserve and gotten permission to leave Gayzer in the turtle habitat. When they arrived, everyone piled out of the car. Samantha took Gayzer back from Sophie and was surprised to see that instead of his normal greenish brown color, he was now covered in bright red and purple heart stickers. "Sophie!" she said to her little sister, "What have you done to Gayzer?"

"I tagged him!" Sophie said smugly. Samantha started to take the stickers off. "NO!" yelled Sophie, "If you take them off how will be know which one is Gayzer?"

This was something Samantha hadn't thought of. There were other box turtles in the pen. "I saw it on the Discovery Channel. You tag animals to know which one is which," Sophie said.

"Oh Sophie, you silly girl," Mom said as she came around the car and caught sight of the turtle. She continued, "Honey, these stickers are not the same as a tag a scientist uses. These stickers wouldn't stay on and if they did they could put

Gayzer in danger. Gayzer looks bumpy and brown and green for a reason. It helps him hide. When Gayzer is in the leaves and sticks on the forest floor, he blends in and it is very hard to see him. He looks just like another pile of leaves. Those stickers are like putting up a flag that says 'Yummy turtle, right here'."

"Oh," said Sophie, "Oops." She and Samantha started taking off the stickers. Sophie said, "But I still want to be sure we can know which one is Gayzer."

"Well, box turtles have lots of little variations," Mom said, "Maybe Gayzer has some way to identify him. Look him over and see if there is something we can use to know it's Gayzer."

The girls looked closely at the turtle.

For the most part he just looked turtle-ish. Then Samantha noticed right at the front of his shell he had a little hole all the way through, as if he had once had a big earring there. "Look, there's a hole in his shell," she pointed out to Sophie. Finding the hole made everyone feel much better. Now it was easy to tell which one was Gayzer, and they didn't even need red and purple heart stickers. Samantha carried Gayzer over toward his new home.

Chapter 11

Home, Sweet Box Turtle, Home

The turtle habitat at the Nature Preserve was a little area in the edge of the forest that had a low fence around it. For the most part, it looked just like the rest of the woods, except there was a small pond about the size of a baby swimming pool in the middle. The pond had a little fountain in it that was shaped like a turtle spitting water out of its mouth. There was also a bunch of big rocks and a half rotten log lying on its side. To Gerti, it looked rather unimpressive. "Will Gayzer be safe in there?" Gerti asked when she saw there was no roof on the pen. The run-in with the cat earlier had her concerned about his safety.

Samantha's Mom thought about it. "Gerti, how many turtles do you see in this pen?" she asked.

Gerti peered at the habitat and said, "None, it looks empty."

"That's what helps to keep them safe here. This pen has lots of turtle hiding spots. There is extra pine straw put in so they can dig down. That log over there is placed so they can get underneath it and the rocks around the pond make lots of hidey holes. If you can't see something, then it's hard to eat it," Mom told her.

Then Mom walked around, staring closely at the ground inside the turtle habitat as she went. Finally she reached down and pulled back a clump of pine straw where the ground looked like it was bumped up a bit. She revealed a hole underneath. After covering it back up, she moved on and pulled back another clump of pine straw. As Gerti watched, Sam's Mom rummaged around in the pine straw until she uncovered a turtle under one of the clumps.

"Here Gerti, hold this one," she said as she handed the newfound turtle to Gerti. Gerti was still getting used to the idea that touching a turtle was a good experience, but she held him bravely. This one was a little larger than Gayzer and a lighter brown color. He was friendly and looked around to see who was holding him.

"Hi, turtle dude," Gerti whispered. The turtle looked back at her with wide reddish brown eyes. Gerti smiled. Meanwhile, Samantha's Mom had uncovered another turtle that had been hiding under the edge of a log.

"Here Sophie, you can hold this one," Mom said, giving the turtle to Sam's little sister. Sophie was happy to take him. This one was smaller than Gayzer. He was also really shy and stayed closed up in his shell. It was a good thing he did too, because Michelle toddled over and snatched the turtle right out of Sophie's hands.

"Tuttle!" Michelle giggled and ran away while Sophie and their Mom chased after her to rescue the poor turtle.

Samantha took over the turtle search. She came to the nature preserve a lot and knew all of their hiding places. Looking for the turtles was like one of those hidden picture games for her. You have to look closely to see the clues to where they were. It wasn't long until Samantha came back holding yet another turtle. "See," she said, "These guys have been living here safely for years. They know how to hide to stay out of trouble. Plus the way their shell closes up makes it really tough to eat them, so they aren't easy prey."

"Years? How long do box turtles live?" Gerti asked. She had thought because they were so small, they probably didn't live that long.

"This little guy could outlive you Gerti," Samantha's Mom said. She had caught Michelle and had the stolen box turtle safely in hand. The turtle was still firmly in his shell. He was pulled in so tightly you couldn't see any head or legs at all.

Sophie gave Michelle a rock and told her it could be a pretend turtle. Mom handed the real turtle back to Sophie and continued, "Box turtles have been known to live to be over 100 years old. You can come back and visit Gayzer and his friends for a long time. When you grow up and have children, you can bring them to see Gayzer." She smiled at that thought.

Gerti felt better, but she still wasn't sure. "The Nature Preserve has indoor cages, doesn't it? Wouldn't it still be just a little safer to keep them inside? Just to be extra careful?" Gerti asked. Samantha was excited that Gerti cared about the turtles and she had become attached to Gayzer too. Suddenly keeping him inside did sound like a safer idea.

"Actually Gerti, he's safer out here. A predator wouldn't get him in a cage inside, but he would have other problems that would be just as deadly. Box turtles are wild animals and are meant to live in a forest. They need a lot of different things it would be hard to give them in a cage," Mom answered.

"Like what?" the girls asked.

"For one thing, they need sunlight. Sunlight has special things called UVB rays in it that helps the turtle make calcium for his bones and his shell. If he doesn't get sunlight, his bones get mushy."

"Ewe. Gross," Sophie said as she made a squishy face and stuck her tongue out to illustrate her point.

"For another thing, turtles need to have a space with lots of different temperatures. Out here they can sit in the sun or go in the shade. They can also dig down under the pine straw or climb up on a rock depending on how they feel. It's hard to get a cage just so and make sure they have all the right spaces they need. Not to mention the things like wild mushrooms and wild insects they are able to catch to eat out here," Mom was just getting started.

"OK, OK, we get it. Wild animals should live in the wild," Samantha interrupted her.

"Yep, it's sad for us, but good for them," Mom replied, "Now everyone show me your turtles." Gerti, Sophie and Samantha held up the turtles they were holding. Michelle held up her rock. Mom snapped a photo to capture the moment.

Mom helped everyone put each of the turtles back in their pen carefully. The girls all watched as each of the turtles slowly walked around the pen and found a hiding spot. It didn't take long for each of them to disappear. Even Gayzer seemed to be right at home. Samantha felt good about leaving him there and left a few apple slices so the turtles would have a snack later on.

On the way home Samantha and Gerti sat beside each other in the back seat.

"That was fun," Gerti said.

Sam smiled smugly and replied, "Yep."

"You find animals a lot, huh?"

"Yep."

"So what do you think we'll find next?"

Quiz Time

Were you paying attention? All the answers to these questions are in the story...

Why did Samantha care which side of the road Grampi was going to put the turtle down on?

How long did Samantha's Mom say that box turtles can live?

What did Gayzer eat in the classroom?

Was there anything Gayzer would **not** eat?

Are box turtles reptiles?

Why did Mrs. Klutz tell the children to be careful where they stepped when looking for Gayzer?

Why do box turtles have hard shells?

Why was it a bad idea to put stickers on Gayzer before they left him in the habitat outside?

Box Turtle Fun Facts

- Turtles are reptiles. All reptiles breath air, and have skin covered in scales or scutes. Most reptiles, including turtles, lay eggs. Reptiles are also "cold–blooded" which means they use their environment to control their body temperature. For instance, they may sit on a rock in the sun to warm up, or go in the water or shade to cool off.

- After maturity (which means they are adult turtles), turtles do not appear to age as they grow older. They are more likely to die from a predator, loss of habitat, or being hit by a car than to die from old age.

- Box turtles can live to be over 100 years old.

- Box turtles are omnivores and will eat almost anything they can find including earthworms, insects, fruit, mushrooms, vegetation, and even dead animals.

- When box turtles are young they will eat more meat and insects, after they are full-grown they eat mostly fruits and vegetation.

- The top shell of a turtle is called the carapace. Eastern box turtles have a tall dome shaped carapace.

- The bottom shell of a turtle is called the plastron. The plastron of a box turtle has a hinge which allows the turtle to completely close its shell.

- Turtles can **not** take off their shells. The shell is as much a part of the turtle as your skin is of you.

- When a turtle's shell is hurt or injured it can heal. Even turtles with lots of damage to their shells have survived and had the shells re-form. A damaged box turtle's shell can also be repaired by veterinarians.

- Box turtles burrow down in the leaf litter to hide from enemies and also to get warmer or colder.

- Mother box turtles will dig a hole and lay eggs down in the hole. Then the mother turtle carefully covers the eggs with dirt and leaf litter. When the eggs hatch the baby box turtles dig their way out.

This story was inspired by a real live box turtle named Gayzer. Gayzer was truly rescued from the middle of the road in Auburn, AL on Gay street by 3 little girls and their grandparents. He now lives at the Louise Kreher Forest Ecology Preserve in Auburn. The other parts of the story are fiction. If you want to meet Gayzer, he is living in a turtle habitat on the Preserve with several other box turtles. You can tell which one is Gayzer because he has a little round hole right through his shell on the front.

For more information on box turtles and other animals in Samantha's adventures go to www.samsanimals.info

Continue the fun with Samantha in book #2!

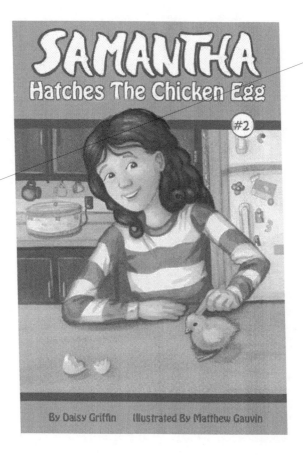

About the Author
Daisy Griffin

When she is not rescuing animals from the many things they can get into on their own, she and her husband are raising three children, who are as much or more interested in creatures as she is. While all the Samantha Stories are works of fiction they all start with an animal found in real life. You can find more information online at www.samsanimals.info.

Proof

Made in the USA
Charleston, SC
17 July 2012